Allan MacDonell

The North-West Transportation, Navigation and Railway Company

SALZWASSER
VERLAG

Allan MacDonell

The North-West Transportation, Navigation and Railway Company

Reprint of the original.

1st Edition 2023 | ISBN: 978-3-37514-636-8

Verlag (Publisher): Salzwasser Verlag GmbH, Zeilweg 44, 60439 Frankfurt, Deutschland
Vertretungsberechtigt (Authorized to represent): E. Roepke, Zeilweg 44, 60439 Frankfurt, Deutschland
Druck (Print): Books on Demand GmbH, In de Tarpen 42, 22848 Norderstedt, Deutschland

THE

NORTH-WEST TRANSPORTATION

NAVIGATION,

AND

RAILWAY COMPANY:

Its Objects.

—————

WM. McD. DAWSON, ESQ., M. P. P. · · · · · PRESIDENT.
LEWIS MOFFAT, ESQ., · · · · · · · · VICE-PRESIEDNT.

DIRECTORS:

Sir ALLAN N. MacNab, Bart.
ALLAN MacDonell, Esq.
JOHN McMurrich, Esq.
GEORGE Munro, Esq.
WM. McMaster, Esq.
E. J. Richardson, Esq.
ANGUS D. Macdonell, Esq.
Thomas Dick, Esq.
J. G. Brown, Esq.
Adam Wilson, Esq.
Viscount Bury.
Kivas Tully, Esq.

J. G. Chapais, Esq., M. P. P.
G. H. Simard, Esq., M. P. P.
John M'Leod, Esq., M. P. P.
Ignace Gill, Esq., M. P. P.
George Michie, Esq.
Wm. P. Howland, Esq., M. P. P.
J. E. Turcotte, Esq., M. P. P.
George Gladman, Esq.
Clark Ross, Esq.
Wm. Kennedy, Esq.
Alfred Roche, Esq.

After first General Meeting of Shareholders, the Board of Directors to be reduced
to ten.

SECRETARY, · · · · · · · ANGUS D. MacDonell, ESQ.
SOLICITOR, · · · · · · · ADAM WILSON, Esq.
BANKERS, · · · · · · · The Bank of Upper Canada.

———

By ALLAN MACDONELL, Esq.

———

TORONTO:
PRINTED BY ORDER OF THE BOARD, BY LOVELL AND GIBSON, YONGE ST.
1858.

INTRODUCTION.

The scheme of opening a communication for traffic and trade from the Atlantic to Pacific shores, through Canada and the North West Territories of British America, has long occupied the attention, and engaged the humble exertions of the writer of these pages. When the project was first placed before the public, it was denounced by many of those who now appear its advocates, as impracticable, and its projectors wild and visionary. It was viewed rather as an hallucination to amuse for a moment and then to vanish ; nevertheless, in despite of all ridicule and opposition, it has been steadily kept before the public since the year 1847, an extract from the communications in a city paper of that year, will exhibit the views then advanced by its correspondent.

"Our portion of this continent of North America, lies directly in the way of the commerce passing between Europe and Asia ; with a ship canal of six hundred and thirty eight yards around the falls of the Sault Sainte Marie, (twenty-one feet in all of height.) We have, through our own territories, the most magnificent inland ship navigation in the world, carrying us one half the way across this continent.

"By means of a railway to the Pacific, from the head of this navigation, a rapid and safe communication would be found, by which the commerce of the world would undergo an entire change, Every one must perceive at a glance, that such a road would stand unrivalled in the world."

Between the years 1847 and 1850, three different Bills were successively introduced into the Legislature, for the purpose of chartering a company to construct a canal at the Sault Ste. Marie, and upon each occasion the Bill was thrown out by the Government, notwithstanding that all the preliminary plans, surveys, and estimates had been made; a company actually formed, and the necessary capital subscribed for constructing the work, and the Bill contained a proviso, that the work should be completed within two years and that the Government might assume the works at any moment, upon paying to the company their actual outlay, with a fair per centage thereon. For some unaccountable cause the Government of the day would neither allow the Company to build the canal, nor would they undertake it as a Government measure.

The consequence is, that a canal was built upon the American side, where the difficulties to be encountered in the construction of such a work were immeasurably greater than any presented upon the Canada side, and, therefore, involved an enormous expenditure of money.

That work completed the last link in the chain of ship canals that connects the Atlantic with the head of Lake Superior.

In 1851, an application was made to the Legislature for the Incorporation of a Company, to construct a railroad from Lake Superior through British Teritories to the Pacific Ocean. The Bill was read a second time and referred to a Committee. That Committee reported unfavourably to the granting a charter upon that occasion; and among the chief objectoin to the application of the petition, it was urged, that as the project involved the cession of tracts of land to the Company, it appeared to the Committee, that the consent of the Imperial Government, as well as the consent of the Indian Tribe, and that of the Hudson's Bay Company should first be obtained, so as to leave no room for subsequent dispute.

In 1853 and in 1855, similar applications were again made to the Legislature, for an act of incorporation for the like purpose, as sought for by the petitioners in 1851.

Each application was met at the outset by the objection that the claims advanced by the Hudson's Bay Company would stand in the way of granting a charter.

The advocates of the scheme then found it necessary to establish the fact, that the claim of the Hudson's Bay Company had no foundation in law or in justice, and that their assumption of power over Canadian Territory was usurped and illegal.

The Hudson's Bay Company was arraigned before that tribunal from which there is no escape. The tribunal of public opinion. Public opinion first in Canada, and then in **England,** pronounced against the "monopoly" and emphatically declared that a vast and fertile region should no longer be closed against man's industry and a nations enterprize. It was felt that the time had now arrived when another application could be made to the Legislature, for carrying into effect the long contemplated project, and without the apprehension of its being any longer deemed "premature."

Accordingly, the Bill under which this Company is now chartered, was introduced into the Legislature and enacted a law.

The principle upon which the charter is based is somewhat different from that upon which the Bill of 1851 was sought to be enacted. The present Act may be said to be more comprehensive in its details, for whilst the Company is empowered to acquire and dispose of lands, it is also authorized to engage in all the industrial pursuits of commercial life.

Toronto, 29th September, 1858.

THE NORTH-WEST

TRANSPORTATION, NAVIGATION,

AND

RAILWAY COMPANY.

This Company has been chartered under an Act of the Provincial Legislature of Canada, with a limited liability. The shareholders being chargeable only to the amount of the subscribed stock held by each individually.

The capital stock, $400,000, in shares of $20 each, power is given to increase the capital stock to $800,000. Authority is also given still further to increase the same at the rate of $30,000 for every mile of railway to be constructed.

The powers of the Company are very extensive. In addition to that of trading, they are authorized to acquire and hold real estate, and sell or otherwise dispose of the same; to construct roads, tramways, railways, canals and all other such works as they may deem necessary for carrying on their trade; and also to improve and render navigable channels of water communication;—and upon all such works and improvements to charge and levy tolls upon all passengers, traffic and freight, passing along or over the same. The Company has likewise the right to own, charter, and navigate boats, vessels, and steamers upon Lakes Huron and Superior, and upon all the waters, lakes and rivers, lying to the nortward and to the westward of the latter, thereby offering to their energy and their enterprize, a new and vast field for commercial adventure.

One of the chief objects in the formation of this Company, is that of participating in that important and lucrative trade, which, although emphatically belonging to Canada, has for the last 38 years, been exclusively monopolized by a few traders of the city of London, styled the Hudson's Bay Company. It is not here intended to enter into a history of that trade, which is coeval with the history of Canada, but it may be necessary briefly to allude to it. Its existence and excercise may be divided into three distinct periods of almost equal duration.

The first dates from the time of the French occupancy of Canada, up to 1763, when the trade of that illimitable region, which this Company now proposes to enter upon, had its outlet through Lake Superior.

The second dates from 1763 up to the year 1821, when the trade of that country was chiefly in the hands of the North-west Company of Montreal, and which followed the old route and channels that their predecessors, the French, had pursued.

The third dates from 1821, (the year when the Northwest Company amalgamated with the Hudson's Bay Company,) up to the present period, and during which time the trade has been monopolized, and forced by the Hudson's Bay Company through the more difficult, circuitous and dangerous route to the shores of Hudson's Bay, and thence to England.

By changing the route of transport, the shorter and the better one, via Lake Superior, became unfrequented and its very existence almost forgotten.

The united Companies under the name of the Hudson's Bay Company, then traded without the apprehension of exciting the rivalry of others. No merchant, trading along the Saint Lawrence, witnessed the imports for the west, nor the exports therefrom. That trade was thus kept a secret from the rising generation in Canada,—the productions of which have for so many years past annually poured wealth into the coffers of those who have never contributed one farthing to the revenue of this country.

The North-West Company on the contrary contributed largely to the revenues of Canada. The magnitude of the operations of that Company were enormous. It carried on a most extensive and lucrative trade, making Montreal the centre and depôt of that trade; and traversing Canada in every direction, not only from Montreal to Hudson's Bay, but with their fleets of boats and canoes, crossing the continent through a chain of lakes and rivers, from Montreal to Puget's Sound, and to the Russian possessions within the artic circle, laden with goods and merchandize for Indian natives, and returning with furs for Europe.

The Northwest Company was formed in 1783, upon a joint stock capital of some $40,000. In three or four years after the formation of the Company, the annual value of the trade had reached $600,000 and it continued to increase until the year 1816, when the Hudson's Bay Company appeared upon the field, and, for the first time advanced a claim to the right of exclusive trade in virtue of an old charter of Charles II. which in truth and in fact conferred no such right.

The Northwest Company had pioneered the way in every instance, and this assumption of an illegal claim, being resisted by the Nortwest Company led to a bloody strife during the four succeeding years, each Company sacrificed trade to carry on the bitter feud, and consequently lost money.

In the year 1821, as above referred to, the two Companies united. From that time Canadian interests were sought to be crushed out, and the revenues arising to Canada from the trade altogether ceased.

The North-West Company gave employment to about 4,000 Canadians : and the wealth that Company realized was freely flung back to circulate in Canada amid the varied industrial pursuits which a trade like theirs had called into action.

In that year, 1821, a license of exclusive trade, was procured from the Imperial Government by the Hudson's Bay Company and the partners of the North West Company conjointly, over certain portions of territory, to which the pretended charter of Charles II could not be made applicable. This license of exclusive trade was, in fact, the origin of the exercise of claim to exclusive monopoly. This license of exclusive trade will expire in, May 1859; it is hoped never again to be renewed.

Since the route of transit has been changed from Lake Superior to Hudson's Bay, time, and the wealth, and the influence of the Hudson's Bay Company has, as it were, obliterated from the mind of Canadians that a North West Company had ever existed, or that such a trade had ever been.

Aided by the wonderful improvements and facilities for transport both in navigation and land carriage, undreamed of by the enterprising traders of those former times, the present company propose to revive that trade and freely exercise those rights which former traders enjoyed during the half century immediately following the conquest of Canada.

To carry on their trade, the North West Company had chains of posts at various distances apart, extending from Montreal, along the rivers and lakes to the head of lake Superior, and thence the chain continued to the shores of the Pacific. The Hudson's Bay Company now occupy and possess most of these posts.

Fort William at the head of Lake Superior, was the chief depôt for the trade of the west, and when so under the North West Company, it frequently contained some 3,000 traders and others. To lay down the annual supply of goods at that locality, cost the North West Company some £30,000; the same quantity of goods can now be laid down there for the sum of £250 or £300. A steamer may now take them from Montreal, or they may be shipped in London and without breaking bulk transhipped at Fort William.

The trade was confined to the skins of wild animals only. A greater traffic than that company enjoyed, is now offered to the merchant and trader of the present day. Enterprise will grasp it and give an unlimited extent to Canadian industry, and to British commerce.

The North West Company had in their employment the most scientific men, that could then be engaged in the explorations and surveys of the whole country from the eastern shore of lake Superior to the shore of the Pacific, and northward to the Arctic seas. We have the benefit of these surveys and explanations, made and continued from the year 1790 up to the year 1821.

We have, likewise, the benefit of more recent researches and surveys made by order of the Imperial Government, and also by order of the Colonial Government under the efficient inspection of Mr. Dawson, brother to the President of this Company.

RESOURCES OF TRADE.

The Hudson's Bay Company make all their importations and all exportations via Hudson's Bay; even their imports to and exports from Lakes Superior and Huron are made via Hudson's Bay.

Their ships do not leave England for Hudson's Bay before the month of June, as they cannot pass through the Hudson's Straits until July, and sometimes not until August, and the goods destined for Lake Superior do not arrive there until the month of August or September. Goods viâ the St. Lawrence and the lakes, can be laid down on Lakes Huron and Superior by the month of May, and may be transported thence to the shores of Hudson's Bay itself by the mouth of June. Thus they would reach Hudson's Bay before the goods destined for that locality could even have left England.

The goods viâ Hudson's Bay destined for the Red River country, and for the Saskatchewan, and the interior country, do not reach the place of their destination until the second year after leaving England.

Goods may be laid down at the Red River via Lake Superior by the month of June, and before the end of that month on the Saskatchewan or almost at any post in the north or west by the beginning of July.

The yearly value of the importations by the Hudson's Bay Company viâ Hudson's Bay, average about $300,000. Their exportation in exchange viâ the same route, varies from $1,000,000 to $2,500,000.

At the half yearly sale in London in April last the proceeds from the trade, it is said, amounted to $1,150,000. The value of the exports are therefore shewn to be as 5 to 1 over the imports.

The route by which these goods are taken to the interior from the shores of Hudson's Bay is only adapted to a boat or canoe navigation, interrupted by numerous and difficult portages. It is a route which forbids the possibility of using steamboats or any other facilities for the transport of merchandise. The distance from York Factory, on Hudson's Bay, where the goods are landed, is about 834 miles to the Red River. The cost of transporting a ton of goods by this route is about £32 10s. or $160, besides the length of time required for the transit.

The rapid advance of the Western United States along the Mississippi and along the banks of the Red River has afforded to the hitherto isolated settlers in the adjoining Canadian territory opportunities of procuring there further supplies of goods

and merchandise which are required by the settler but which
are not supplied by the Hudson's Bay Company. Accordingly
a land route has been established between the Red River Settlement and St. Paul's in Minnesota, over a distance of some 600
miles.

The traffic is carried on by means of carts, each cart carries
about 700 lbs. weight. The time occupied in transit from the
Red River to St. Paul's is from twenty to thirty days, and a like
time is occupied in returning.

The route is intersected by lakes and rivers across which the
carts and the merchandise must be ferried over and the cattle
swam across.

This mode of conveyance involves not only the labor of many
men and cattle, but a loss of nearly three months at the most
important season of the year to the settler for action at home.
The cost for transport is at the rate of $42 to $45 per cart or
about $120 per ton. Upwards of 500 carts went from the Red
River to St. Paul's this last summer and carried with them about
$180,000 worth of furs.

The goods taken back in exchange in all probability would
average about the same value but be of much greater weight,
and consequently cost more for the transport by the carts than
did the furs.

Besides there is a duty paid upon the furs when passing into
American territory, and also a duty paid upon some of the
articles taken in exchange, which would not be the case if passing viâ Lake Superior, through British territory.

Thus, notwithstanding the present difficulties of transportation, it is seen that a large trade has sprung into existance,
although it is but confined to the fur trade, and which as regards
the transit to St. Paul's may be said only to be in its infancy.
The following extract from a Report of a Select Committee of
the Legislature of Minnesota, published by order of the House
of Representatives in the month of August last past, will suffice
to shew the value anticipated to arise from the traffic with the
British possessions along the Red River, &c. : —

"Simultaneously with the movements in this city and in the
different parts of the State for the establishment of an emigrant
route through Minnesota and the British possessions to the new

field of adventure on Frazer River, the opportune arrival of some six hundred carts from the Red River laden with the furs of that region, had the effect of directing public attention more immediately to the growing importance of our commercial relations with these remarkable settlements, while it furnished at the same time a multitude of witnesses not only to the advantages of the proposed route, but to the richness of the resources which such a route would develope. And to the beauty and fertility of the region tributary to the valley of the Mississippi, which it would open to colonization.

"The novel appearance of the visitors themselves, the odd uniformity of their costume of course blue cloth, with its barbaric opulence of brass buttons and fanciful ostentation of red belts. The strange mixture of complexions which they presented, all the way down from the fair skin and light soft curls of the Celt to the dingy colour and straight black hair of the Indian, with every intermediate shade which the amalgamation of races could produce. Their language as various as their origin, a curious medley of Chippewa, Cree, French, English, and Gaelic; their rude wooden carts guiltless of iron, even to the veriel piccadello of a nail; drawn for the most part by oxen harnessed singly in shafts, with gearing made of strips of raw hide; and filing in long procession through the streets of the city with the disciplined sequence of an Asiatic caravan. It is not surprising that these incidents of social life, removed at once from barbarism and civilization, should have excited some interest in the history of a people who, with the marks of a European extraction, emerge from the depths of the wilderness with the characteristics of the savage."

The report goes on to state, "These carts like the marine tonnage in a particular trade afford a valuable measure of the growth of that trade." Besides this, the average of annual exports of furs from the Company's possessions alone will be about $1,800,000. The annual imports of the Company's goods into the Red River Settlement alone have averaged for a number of years past $100,000. It is reasonable to presume that at least an equal amount (a very low estimate) is distributed among the numerous posts along the Saskatchewan and its tributaries.

The proportion then of the whole export of furs from the basin of the Winnipeg may be safely estimated at one half of the whole trade of the Company, or at the least $1,000,000. Such are the proceeds of the trade in its present restricted state, and in one class of commodities alone. What will it be when left to the free course of commercial competition, and when an unrestricted colonization opens new fields of industry and presses all the resources of a new western world into the stream of reciprocal intercourse whose swelling volume is already wearing a deep track between Red River and St. Paul's.

It is notorious that the Hudson's Bay Company do not import a fifth part of what the country requires and can pay for. By the construction of roads and the improvement of the inland navigation, and carrying in settlers, this Company will develop the great resources of that countrys wealth and be enabled to trade in all the varied productions which man's industry and knowledge creates.

From the shores of Lake Huron to those of the Pacific the Hudson's Bay Company have a series of trading forts or chief depôts upon which smaller posts are again dependent. Each chief fort has therefore dependent upon it for supplies the number of Indians as shewn in the annexed table, taken from appendix C in the evidence adduced before the Committee of the House of Commons upon the Hudson's Bay Company in the month of July of the past year, shewing the number of Indians dependent upon them for supplies:

Lake Huron.

La Cloche Fort	150
Little Current	500
Mississaga, 150 ; Green Lake, 150	300
White Fish Lake, 150 ; Sault Ste. Marie, 150	300
(At the latter should be set down 300.)	
Lake Nipissing	350

Lake Superior.

Balchewaana, 100 ; Mamainse, 50	150
Michipicoten, 300 ; Pic, 110 ; Nepigon, 250	650
Fort William, 350 ; Pigeon River, 50	400
Lac la Pluie, Fort Francis	1500
Fort Alexander, 300 ; Rat Portage, 500	800
White Dog, 100 ; Lac du Bonnet, 50	150
Lac des Bois, 200 ; Shoal Lake, 200	400
Assiniboine, Red River, Winipeg, &c.	10000

The bands along the Saskatchewan, &c., are denominated the tribe of the Plains, and are dependent for supplies as follows :

At Fort Edmonton, 7,500 ; Carleton House, 6,000....... 13500
Fort Pitt, 7,000 ; Mountain House, 6,000................. 13000

North and west of the Saskatchewan and along the slopes of the Rocky Mountains, the tribes are styled the Thick Wood Indians, and these number about 35,000.

The Indians in British Oregon, and along the northwest coast number about 80,000. The whole total half breeds and Indians in what is called the Hudson's Bay Territories, and depending for supplies upon the Hudson's Bay Company, are set down as amounting to at least 158,000. Here is a population which must create a vast demand for Canadian manufactures and importations of British goods, all which can be so much more advantageously supplied to them viâ Lake Superior.

To supply this population, it has been shewn that the Hudson's Bay Company take into the country, upon an average only $300,000 worth of goods, something over $1.80 per head. Each Indian, upon an average, would take $40 worth of goods, per annum, and the country possess resources wherewith to pay for them.

The goods and merchandize which an Indian requires are various, such as guns, blankets, cottons, clothing of all kinds, powder, shot, tobacco, teas, flour, &c., these two latter articles of barter are never introduced by the Hudson's Bay Company, into many parts of the country whence they derive a vast profit.

Taking the estimate at $40 per head would shew a demand exists for $6,160,000 worth of importations, where $300,000 worth are now only supplied. But let us calculate at $10 per head, *a very low estimate*, and we have a demand for $1,580,-000 of imports.

The Hudson's Bay Company trade only for furs, and for their imports of $300,000, they export from $1,500,000 to $2,800,-000, or at the rate of 500 per cent. of profit upon their imports.

And yet their are various other productions, which can be made as profitable sources of trade as the furs of wild animals. Take, for instance, the buffalo, of which the hunters from the Red River Settlement alone, kill annually 25,000. Each animal will, upon an average, produce from 50 ℔s to 70 ℔s of tallow.

Let us take the average, however, at 40 ℔s per animal, 25,000 at 40℔s equal 1,000,000 ℔s, this at 10 cents per pound, $1,000,000; hides, at $3 each, $75,000, making $175,000.

The tongues, the beef, &c., if cured for exportation or trade, would produce a much greater amount, say $400,000, making $575,000 worth of trade in addition to the fur trade. Time and again efforts have been made by some of the settlers at the Red River, to embark in the tallow trade, but the Hudson's Bay Company have invariably refused to export the same, either through an inability to do so, or through a desire to prohibit a traffic which would militate against their monopoly of the fur trade.

It is estimated that upwards of 150,000 buffalo are annually slaughtered in the valley of the Saskatchewan, thousands of these wantonly, and as many killed only for their tongues.

When the Indians would find that the carcase, the tallow, the horns, and even the hoofs would procure the necessaries of life, just as readily as furs, a most important trade will have sprung into existence.

100,000 buffalo would be as readily procured, as the 25,000 by the Red River hunters, those estimated at the same calculation, as given above, would produce a trade worth $2,300,000, which in addition to the estimated fur trade now enjoyed by the Hudson's Bay Company, in that section of country alone, would swell its value upwards of $3,300,000.

We import and pay large sums of money for these very articles of production, which are peculiar to our own country, and, stranger still, we import the very furs from England which have been exported from this country, via Hudson's Bay.

We import annually:

Fur goods, value $169,572, duty thereon, $24,076...$193,648.
Fur undressed, no duty thereon .... 50,624.
Tallow..360,000.
Hides..259,000.
Fish oil .... 249,000.
                                                                ──────────
     Total .... $1,112,996.

With exception of those furs that are imported from England the residue of the above imports are all from the United States.

Immense fisheries for oil may be carried on in Hudson's Bay, distant from Lake Superior about 300 miles, viâ the Michipicotan river, along which route all the merchandize and goods of the Hudson's Bay Company, destined for Lakes Huron and Superior, are now brought from Hudson's Bay.

Apart from these other productions of the country, which may be rendered articles of vast traffic, immense quantities of salt may be had in various sections of the country, equal to the best. Inexhaustible beds of mineral pitch abound, all which will become articles of traffic so soon as facilities for transport are created, and opportunities offered for successfully engaging in the above important trades.

The superior advantages which the old route from the western side of Lake Superior possesses for making the whole trade of the north and west tributary to it are so immeasurably greater, that so soon as it shall be reopened and a highway perfected for the conveyance of traffic, trade and passengers, the Hudson's Bay Company, and all others holding trading or other connections either with the Arctic shores or the coasts of the Pacific, can only compete for the trade by transit along the route proposed.

The mining for gold upon Frazer River, and the establishment of a new British Colony on the west side of the Rocky Mountains, will give a stimulous to immigration as well from the old country as from the various portions of the United States and of Canada.

This is a most important consideration for the immediate carrying into operation the works of the Company, as it will be enabled to afford to immigrants and others seeking those new fields of industry and enterprise, or even to those seeking southern Oregon in the United States, the safest, easiest, speediest, and the cheapest route that can possibly be established. From the conveyance of passengers alone a large profit may reasonably be anticipated to arise.

To provide the facilities for transport it is proposed as soon as possible to establish a line of railway from the shores of Lake Superior to the eastern end of Lac la Pluie by either one of two routes, as shall be judged most advisable, after a careful and thorough examination. One has been already surveyed, the

B

other is in the course of being so. This latter route would pass from Lake Superior to White Fish Lake, and thence beyond it along a chain of navigable waters leading to Lac la Pluie, the distance requiring about 140 miles of Railway.

The other proposed line is about 30 miles to the northward and leads from Lake Superior to Dog Lake, and thence along the chain of navigable waters between it and Lac la Pluie. The distance by this route would involve the construction of about 185 miles of railway.

At the western extremity of Lac la Pluie is the entrance to the Lac la Pluie River. To make perfect the navigation between the lake and the river a short canal of 8 chains in length, with two locks of about 11 feet lift each, is necessary. This would afford a steamboat navigation from the eastern end of Lac la Pluie to the western extremity of the Lake of the Woods, a distance of about 180 miles.

Instead of pursuing the route offered by the river Winnipeg, which would involve not only a more circuitous route but considerable lockage. It is proposed to construct a railroad from the western side of the Lake of the Woods to the Red River, a distance of less than 100 miles.

The portion of country over which this railway will pass is singularly adapted to the work, a long section of the line may be said to be naturally graded and will pass along a gravel ridge well calculated materially to assist in the construction of a waggon road or a railway. No right of way being required to be purchased, and the country along which the whole line of this section of road will pass being so well adapted for the project, the expense of construction must be very far below the cost usually incurred upon such works.

Under their charter the Company are authorised to increase their capital stock at the rate of $30,000 for every mile of railway to be constructed.

The Company are therefore enabled to increase their capital stock for the 240 miles of railway now contemplated to be built to a farther sum of $7,200,000, a sum of money sufficient for the purpose.

When those lines of railway shall have been completed and the navigation improved between Lac la Pluie and the Lake of the Woods, the distance between Lake Superior and the Red River will be made in less than 24 hours.

Steamboats may even now navigate the Red River from its mouth to upwards of 100 miles beyond the boundary line at Pambina, and the river is capable of being made navigable for steamers as far up as Breakenside, a distance of 450 miles from its mouth ; thus in a great measure rendering tributary to the proposed line the vast and rapidly increasing immigration and trade of the Western United States of America.

The same steamboats may run from the Red River into and through Lake Winnipeg and thence up the Saskatchewan to the first rapid in that river, thus affording an uninterrupted steamboat navigation for over 750 miles. The obstruction at the mouth of the Saskatchewan involves only the short distance of three miles, and until a canal shall be constructed there, another line of steamers will be necessary to ply above the rapids. A steamer from the Red River will be hauled over the portage and placed upon the river above it. The Saskatchewan is then navigable by either branch to the very foot of the Rocky Mountains.

To the immense emigration now passing from the older portions of the United States into Washington Territory and Southern Oregon, the south branch will afford the easiest, the shortest, and the cheapest route for passengers or traffic. This south branch rises within the territories of Western United States, and is navigable to almost its source. Thus the American immigration would pass through St. Paul's to Breakenridge on the Red River, thence down the Red River and via Winnipeg and the south branch of the Saskatchewan, reach the place of their destination almost the whole way by water through British territory.

The north branch will offer a steamboat navigation to within about 200 miles of Frazer's River, or the centre of British Columbia. No portion of the Continent of America affords such facilities for being made the highway of nations between Europe and Asia as does the line of communication now proposed to be opened for traffic and trade.

The facilities of Atlantic communication are now such that the workshops and manufactories of Britain may almost be said to be anchored in the currents of the St. Lawrence. From Montreal the time of transit would be as follows:

Montreal to Toronto 15 hours, by railroad; from Toronto to head of Lake Superior, 90 miles by railroad, the rest by first class steamers, fifty-six hours; from Lake Superior, by railroad and by steamer, to Red River, 24 hours; from Red River by steamboat to Carleton House on the Saskatchawan, 600 miles at 10 miles an hour, 60 hours; Carlton House to Edmonton House by steamer, 400 miles, 40 hours. This is the head of navigation on the Saskatchewan.

The head waters of the Saskatchewan and Frazer's River rise within a short distance of each other. The locality between them forms the well known pass between Mount Hooker and Mount Brown, which is now readily traversed on horseback. The journey from Edmonton to the junction of Frazer's and Thompson's Rivers, occupies 5 days.

At the western side of this pass is a long stretch of fertile land sloping down to Thompson's and Frazer's Rivers. This pass between Mount Hooker and Mount Brown is in a direct line to the gold fields now attracting so much attention, as it is also the direct road to Victoria.

This pass through the mountains has been traversed hundreds of times by individuals, who represent that a road through it can be constructed with less difficulty and even at a less expense than will be required in some parts of the line between Lake Superior and Lac la Pluie. Taking the distances as stated above:—Lake Superior to Red River, 400 miles rail and steamer, 24 hours; Red River to Carlton House, 600 miles, 60 hours; Carleton House to Edmonton, 400 miles, 40 hours; Edmonton to junction of Frazer's and Thompson's River, 200 miles, 20 hours; making the whole distance in six days from Lake Superior, calculating at 10 miles per hour. Making the calculation at 14 miles an hour would not be an unreasonable one, this would give the time about 4½ days, to which adding about 3½ days for travel from Montreal to the head of Lake Superior, would make 8 days to Frazer's River or British Columbia.

Fourteen miles per hour is perhaps the extreme rate of speed, but it is perfectly attainable and at a moderate expense.

Again, taking the route from New York we will find the line proposed offers an almost similar speed either to Frazer's River or Washington Territory : New York to Prairie du Chien, by railroad, 60 hours ; Prairie du Chien to St. Paul's, 300 miles by steamer, 21 hours ; St. Paul's to Breakenridge on the Red River, 200 miles land travel by stage, 56 hours ; Breakenridge to mouth of Red River, 450 miles by steamboat, 33 hours ; thence to Edmonton (as above), 106 hours. Thus from New York in 13 days, or for passage by the south branch of the Saskatchawan into Washington Territory about the same time would be required.

It needs no prophetic inspiration to foretel it, that so soon as this proposed communication is opened, speedily will be developed an inland inter-oceanic communication between the Pacific and Atlantic shores via our inland ship navigation to the head of Lake Superior ; a line of route which must soon bear upon its smooth and peaceful surface the golden harvests of the mineral slopes of the Pacific coast, and the rich freights of China and of India.

The superior advantages which the route will afford not only for communication between Europe, America and Asia, but the great facilities it will afford for postal communication throughout the British Empire will no doubt be taken advantage of to the enhancement of the profits of the Company.

The North-West Transportation, Navigation and Railway Company cannot be a monopoly. A large proportion of the anticipated profits are calculated to arise from the opening a cheap and speedy communication between Lake Superior and that vast and fertile wilderness which offers resources to all industry. and is a refuge from all want. Every individual who may pass along the route, either as a passenger, a trader, or a settler becomes a consumer or a producer, or he is both, thus, while the Company will profit by a passenger trafic or by the conveyance of goods and merchandize, imports and exports, the progress and prosperity of Canada must be advanced. Her revenues multiplied an hundred fold by the additional demands which an increasing population always creates, and consequently a competition in trade.

The immediate object of the Company is at once to enter into trade by forming a chain of establishments from the shores of Lake Superior to the interior, and these will be extended as circumstances require. Thus affording the best means of speedily opening a transport communication between Lake Superior and the Red River, with the view of ultimately opening a direct transit communication thence to the shores of the Pacific.

The communication to be made by water in the first instance —as far as it can be made available.

The construction of roads, tramways, railways and canals will only be undertaken as our necessities require, and as the growth of traffic demands increased facilities.

These will be constructed not so much with a view of deriving a profit from the toll to be levied upon them, as for the object of affording facilities for the transport of the traffic and trade of the Company, and of all others who may adventure in the trade of the country.

It is the interest of the Company to encourage traffic and trade, to promote immigration, carry passengers and merchandise, and supply present and future settlers with all the necessaries of life. A great object will therefore be to afford facilities and encouragement for an inmigrant population entering into the country as speedily as possible, at a moderate rate per head; with this view favorable localities will from time to time be selected throughout the country for establishments, where all the necessaries of life can be readily and cheaply procured. As some time must elapse before the proposed lines of railway between Lake Superior and Lac la Pluie, and the Lake of the Woods and Red River can under the most favorable circumstances be accomplished. It is proposed for the present to avail ourselves of the facilities afforded by water communication, as well for the purpose of trade and transport as for carrying forward the material for the construction of small steamers to ply upon the long reaches of navigable waters which lie westward of the height of land, these in turn will carry or transport the materials necessary for the construction of good waggon roads which will be built along the proposed lines of railway, as a preparatory step to commencing such works.

It is obvious that in the early stages of working a transportation company it is all important to use water communications wherever these can be rendered available; it requires but comparatively small outlay, and increased force need only be taken on as the traffic and trade demands it.

Mode of Transportation proposed to be at preset adopted, and until such times as greater facilities are afforded :

Until a railway be built, a good waggon road will be constructed from the shores of Lake Superior, either to Whitefish Lake or to Dog Lake, thence the route will be through the chain of navigable waters leading from either of the above named lakes to Rainy Lake, the proposed terminus of the Railway from Lake Superior. The several portages which interrupt the above mentioned chain of navigable waters will be improved so that laden batteaux carrying about five tons may be hauled across without unloading.

A wooden railway or tramway from the head of the portage to the next clear water will suffice for this. The portages are all short, few of them over 100 yards in length.

This mode of conveyance will enable the company at once to commence operations, and at the same time carry forward the project of constructing good waggon roads, connecting the long reaches of water navigation, whereby the numerous portages will be avoided. It will likewise enable the company to carry out the project of placing steamers upon Lac la Pluie, the River la Pluie, and the Lake of the Woods, as by no other means can the material for the construction of steamers be carried forward. A waggon road will also be constructed from the western side of the Lake of the Woods to the Red River.

These waggon roads are to form the line over which the contemplated railways shall pass. As these roads progress westward from Lake Superior so will the facilities for a more speedy mode of transport increase.

The estimated cost of perfecting a steamboat and waggon road communication between Lake Superior and Frazer River, as shewn by the prospectus issued, is about $300,000. When the projected plan is complete as far as the Red River, the time of travel between Lake Superior and that point will be reduced to four days. The communication from the Red River to Edmonton house as has been already shewn will be by steamer.

Profits to arise from immediately opening a transit communication between Lake Superior and the Red River. A communication capable of taking heavy merchandize, one established between Lake Superior and the Red River, even though it be confined to conveyance by batteaux, will warrant the placing a steamer upon the Red River to ply to the Saskatchewan, or even as far as possible in the direction of the McKenzie River, for although the company are only authorised to construct canals, railways, &c., within the limits of Canada, they are not forbidden to trade beyond these limits.

This Company possessing steamers upon the Red River will under any circumstances be enabled to make tributary to it the carrying trade of all that vast country lying to the westward and the northward of the Red River.

Taking 600 carts as the measure of freightage between Red River and Saint Paul's at the rate of $42 per cart, we have for freightage alone $25,200. It is not unreasonable to suppose that an equal amount is paid for the transportation of goods in returning, thus shewing that there is paid for freight to and from the Red River the sum of $50,400.

This carrying trade must be tributary to the Lake Superior route *even though that route be adapted only for batteaux.* Besides the above, there would be the carriage of the exports and imports of the Hudson's Bay Company, for if they continue in the trade they will be compelled to abandon the route by Hudson's Bay, whenever the Lake Superior route is opened for traffic.

A batteau will carry five tons, and five men will man her, and transport her cargo from the shores of Lake Superior to the Red River in fifteen days, if with favorable weather the trip could be accomplished in much less time, for on the long reaches of water navigation one hundred miles a day can be made, so that in fact the distance might be accomplished in seven days or less. The cost of transport, wages to men at $20 per month, let us say seven men, for fifteen days would give $70 for the transport of five tons, or at the rate of $14 per ton, to which add cost of transport from England to head of Lake Superior $15, making in all $25 to Red River.

The route from Hudson's Bay requires a period of one year for the transit, and at a cost of $160 per ton.

The route from St. Paul's to the Red River requires from twenty to thirty days in transit, and at a cost of $120 per ton, the cost of transport from England to St. Paul's cannot be less than from England to the head of Lake Superior, thus making the cost almost equal to that by Hudson's Bay.

When facilities shall be offered for transport to the Red River *via* Lake Superior, the trade and the traffic on the route will increase at a compound ratio, for with it will advance immigration and all those industrial pursuits which are incidental to the opening new and progressing countries.

This company being a trading company, can accomplish the opening and working the route at far less expense than a company not possessed of trading privileges, inasmuch as the payments to employees, voyageurs and others, will in a great measure be made in the usual course of trade, besides being in other respects consumers of the merchandise of the company, &c.

Sources of immediate profit to the Company arising from trade. Along Lakes Huron and Superior, making a coast line of near 1000 miles. The Hudson's Bay Company maintain six forts or principal trading depôts; upon each one of these several smaller trading posts are dependent, all are sustained by the profits of trade, and yet the company trade in little else than furs. At one or two of the forts that company latterly engaged in the fisheries on the lake. This trade promises to become one of the most important of the industrial pursuits of the lake country. Last year the Americans alone exported some 20,000 barrels, a large proportion of these were taken on our shores principally by Indians and half-breeds, who are generally paid in goods.

A barrel of those fish brings $7 or $8, the cost of putting up a barrel may be from $2 to $4. Trading posts established at convenient localities along these lakes would be resorted to by the Indians who would readily engage in fishing, and receive in payment the goods of the company. It would materially benefit the Indians and all others, by inducing to industrial pursuits where heretofore there has been no encouragement.

The outlay necessary for this branch of trade will be but trifling, and the profits to be derived would be lucrative, and the returns immediate. The spring fishery commences early in

May and will close in June, and a ready market can be found at the Sault St. Marie, and at Chicago.

By at once engaging in this trade, the Indian bands along the coast will be enlisted in the service of the Company, whilst a demand will be created for those goods and necessaries of life which this Company would be so well calculated to supply. It would also enable this Company to carry on their works in the construction of roads, &c., more cheaply and more effectually.

Cured fish could be readily exchanged for those kinds of provisions which will be indispensable for the maintenance of a number of workmen and laborers upon the works.

It is reasonable to anticipate that a fair portion of that trade by which the establishment of the Hudson's Bay Company are maintained will be participated in by this Company, as at least this Company will be enabled to afford their goods, &c., at rates more reasonable than the Hudson's Bay Company, when it is considered that the supplies of the various establishments along the lakes and in the interior, are brought from England *via* Hudson's Bay.

Should these goods hereafter be brought *via* the St. Lawrence, the natural and cheapest channel, this Company would be able to afford greater facilities for their transportation than any other, and in all probability the carriage thereof would be no inconsiderable source of revenue.

It may not be deemed unadvisable, certainly great facilities are offered for establishing a telegraph line in conjunction with the works of this Company.

The announcement of the discovery of gold upon the Frazer's River, and the erection of a new British Province along the Pacific coast, creates the necessity not only of opening the cheapest and best route to these regions, but also of possessing the speediest mode of communication between Great Britain and her new colony.

This project carries with it an unusual degree of importance to the British Empire, when it is considered that through British Columbia facilities are offered for extending this system of communication to the most distant portion of Her Asiatic possessions, thereby consolidating her power and affording an additional guarantee for its perpetuity upon either continent.

In connection with the works of the Company a telegraph line may be carried from this city to Lake Huron, thence along the coast of that Lake and of Lake Superior, and thence westward along the route proposed to Frazer's River, and to its mouth.

From that point it may be carried *via* the Aleutian and the Kurile Islands to the Asiatic coast and along it to China and to India, or the line may run northward and cross at Behring Straits.

In no locality would more than 40 miles of cable be submerged.

Whether the telegraphic cable laid between Galway and Newfoundland be a successful experiment or not, it has clearly demonstrated the fact, that the length of cable to be submerged presents the only formidable difficulty to be encountered in perfecting a telegraphic communication between Europe and America. Should, however, the recent attempt to form such a communication prove to be a failure, it is to be hoped that the enterprise will not be abandoned because that Newfoundland and Galway are pronounced to be too distant from each other for successfully carrying out the scheme or working the line. A more favorable route for forming such communication may be found where the line of cable to be submerged will not exceed 500 miles.

Making the North of Scotland the starting point, thence to the Faroe Isles, thence to Iceland, thence to Greenland and along its southern coast, whence it would pass to Labrador and thence to Quebec.

Thus can a telegraphic communication be had with the seat of Empire from the most distant possessions of the British Crown.

Should the project be entertained of establishing a telegraph line across the Continent in conjunction with the other operations of the Company, it would be necessary to make an application to the Legislature for power to increase the capital stock of the Company for such purpose, and perhaps to ask for a grant of lands to aid in the general undertaking of the Company. The stock of the Company as at present is:

Capital Stock $400,000, to increase $400,000....... $800,000
240 miles of railroad to be built....................... 7,200,000

To carry out the present objects of the Company... $8,000,000

Any further line of railroad which the Company should contemplate building would authorise the Company to still further increase the Capital Stock under their Charter.

APPENDIX.

In the year 1851, a Bill for the Incorporation of a Company to construct a Railroad from the head of Lake Superior through British Territory to the Pacific was introduced into the Legislature and upon its being read a second time was referred to a Committee for Report thereon.

The following Report together with the observations therein alluded to, taken from the Journals of the Legislative Assembly for the year 1851 is here given :

EIGHTH REPORT.

THE Standing Committee on Railways and Telegraph Lines, beg leave to make their Eighth Report :

They have considered the Bill for a Charter to construct a Railway through the British Territories in North America to the Pacific Ocean, and are reluctantly obliged to report that, in their opinion such application is premature, and that the Petitioners have not taken the preliminary steps to entitle them to an Act of Incorporation.

As the project involves the cession to the Company of a large tract of country, it appears to Your Committee, the consent of the Imperial and Provincial Governments should have been first obtained and these claims, as well as those of the Indian Tribes and the Hudson's Bay Company ; to the lands in question, adjusted ; so as to leave no room for subsequent dispute.

In addition to this objection, Your Committee have had no evidence laid before them, of the capacity of the Petitioners to commence or prosecute the undertaking. It does not appear that any capital stock has been subscribed for or paid up, or that the Petitioners are in a position to avail themselves of a charter loan, if granted. Your Committee have already reported their opinion that railway charters should only be granted to. parties who can show their ability and desire, to proceed with their undertaking at once, and with energy and effect, and they adhere to that opinion.

At the same time, Your Committee feel bound to state their impression that the scheme ought not to be regarded as visionary or impracticable. When the project was first suggested in the United States by Mr. Whitney, its novelty and extent led many persons to consider it as such, but that gentleman by his untiring energy and ability, has by degrees led the public mind both in his own country and in England to regard it with favor.

Your Committee are strongly inclined to believe, that this great work, will at some future period, (should this Continent continue to advance as heretofore, in prosperity and population) be undertaken by Great Britain and the United States.

The superior advantages of the route to the Pacific Ocean through the British Territory, has been ably urged on the public attention by Allan McDonnell, Esquire, and others; and Your Committee indulge a hope that the Imperial Government will be led to entertain the subject as one of national concern, and to combine with it, a general and well organized system of colonization.

Your Committee beg leave to append to their report an instructive paper on this subject prepared by Allan McDonell, Esquire.

Your Committee recommend that if Your Honorable House concur in the rejection of the application, the fee paid by the Petitioners, should be refunded.

All which is respectfully submitted.

ALLAN N. MACNAB,
Chairman.

30th August, 1851.

OBSERVATIONS

UPON

THE CONSTRUCTION OF A RAILROAD

FROM

LAKE SUPERIOR TO THE PACIFIC.

BY ALLAN MACDONELL, ESQ.

To shorten, by a Western passage, the route to the Indies, which is now conducted around the fearful barriers of Cape Horn and Southern Africa, is a design that has long occupied the attention and aroused the exertion of all maritime nations. England's exploring expeditions to both the Atlantic and Pacific coasts, have pried into every sinuosity of the shore, from lat. 30°, South, to the borders of the Frigid Zone, and in the defeat of her exertions, projects have been forming to pierce the Continent within the limits of a foreign country, and where England would be placed at the mercy of her rivals. Whilst France, Mexico, the United States, and other Powers, meditate the separation of the Continent at the Isthmus of Panama; let England at least enquire whether she has not, within her own territories, superior facilities for accomplishing the same grand purpose which impel them.

Within this past year, three works have been published in England, emanating from different sources, urging the necessity and advantages of a Railway connection between the Atlantic and Pacific Oceans, such Railway to be constructed through the British Possessions. My present object is not to canvas the schemes proposed by any of these several parties or projectors, whereby they would seek to carry out their views, but if possible, to direct the attention of the Canadian public to the existence of such a project, and the incalculable advantages which must result to this and the Mother Country, could such a connection be accomplished. In one of the pamphlets referred to by Major Smith, the plan proposed by him is to construct such road by convict labour; the others, one by a Mr. Wilson, (who, I believe, was at one time in the employment of the Hudson Bay Company,) and the other by Lieutenant Synge, of the Royal Engineers, I have not met with. That the construction of such a road is feasible and practicable, I have reason to believe, and will propose to build it upon a plan similar to · that proposed by Mr. Whitney, for constructing a like Railway communication through the United States,—which plan is so peculiarly adapted to our country, that it cannot fail of finding as favorable a reception here as it did there. The scheme of building a Railway for hundreds of miles through a country which at present is a wilderness, seems at first sight, absurdly extravagant, as well as utterly impracticable ; and so it would be if the plan contemplated, was one to be fully carried out within any short period of time. It must be borne in mind that under the most favorable circumstances, some years would be required for the construction of such a work ; with its progress, population must keep in advance, or accompany its advancement.

In determining, therefore, upon the wisdom or practicability of constructing such a road, the whole matter is to be looked at prospectively,—the question is not how far the present condition of the country and its interests warrant the undertaking, but whether such a state of things will be likely to exist, as will justify it when it shall have been accomplished. As to the expediency or advantage of constructing such road, I imagine there cannot be a diversity of opinion, if it shall be found to be practicable.

Not only are the United States, but the whole of Europe aroused to the importance of securing the immense trade of China, and the East Indies—even in the days of Hernando Cortes it was thought possible and expedient to unite the two oceans by a ship canal across the Isthmus of Panama, and since that time almost every nation has talked of doing so ; nor is the project at the present time abated or suspended. Even in the early history of this country, the French perseveringly and anxiously sought for a supposed water communication from the St. Lawrence to the Pacific ; with a view to secure if possible, that important trade which has from the earliest history enriched, beyond calculation, every nation that held it, while each in its turn has fallen from power and affluence as it lost or surrendered it. Without adverting to its effects on other nations, it is sufficient to look to England ; she owes more of her grandeur and her power to her commerce with the East Indies, than to almost any other source whatever. At the present time, she is to commerce, what the principle of gravitation is to the material world—that which regulates and upholds all. And yet, should the United States construct a Railway through their territories, she might too soon feel how precarious is her tenure of the sceptre of the seas—it would be wrested from her by her active and energetic rival ; she would be driven from her position, and her Indian fleets as effectively forced from the bosom of the ocean, as have been the caravans which formerly carried across the deserts the wealth of India ; or, as England snatched from Holland the East Indian trade, so in her turn she may be deprived of it by the United States : such would be—such some day may be—the effect produced by a Railroad through the territories of this latter power. It is therefore incumbent upon England, for her own sake, and it becomes her duty and her interest, to inquire into the practicability of constructing such road through British dominions, whereby our active and enterprizing rival will cease to be regarded as such, and a British people will have no competitor for maritime supremacy among nations. If it be practicable to connect the Pacific with the head waters of our inland navigation, it ought not to be delayed. Every facility should be offered for carrying it into effect. It would not only be the means of settling all the lands capable of sustaining population in those regions, but the commercial relations of the world would be altered ; the great West would be penetrated—the streams of commerce would be changed from boisterous seas and stormy capes, to flow to our shores upon the Pacific, and through the depths of our Western wilds. With the power of steam through an accessible region and over a peaceful sea, England would be placed at one-fourth of the distance at which she has hitherto stood, from the treasures of the East ; her merchants would be able to undersell, in their own ports, all the nations of the world. In other words, she would render commerce tributary to them, and Canada would be the great toll-gate through which this enormous traffic must pass. No other route accross the Continent of America could compete with this, as will be shown hereafter; at present, I shall simply point out the route proposed:

Liverpool to St. Lawrence, (miles) 2,800
St. Lawrence to British Boundary, Lake Superior ... 1,150
Lake Superior to Fuca's Straits ...., 1,500
                                                         ―――――
                                                         5,450

The distance from Fuca's Straits to Japan is about 4,000 miles; to Shanghae about 5,000. Vancouver's Island commands the Straits, and abounds with excellent harbours; coal of a superior quality is found there; the Indians mine it and deliver it on board the Hudson Bay Steamers at a mere nominal charge. No part of the Pacific coast affords such capabilities as does this for controlling the whole trade and traffic of the Pacific.

It might be assumed as a certainty, that a cargo from Shanghae, borne by a modern ocean steamer over this placid sea, could be unloaded in fifteen or twenty days, at some one of the harbours at Fuca's Straits, and in from three to five days more, placed for sale or transportation on the banks of Lake Superior. The construction of such a road in the direction of Fuca's Straits, would shorten the distance to England from China, &c., by sixty or seventy days, and place before us a mart of six hundred millions of people, and enable us geographically to command them. Leaving it to the guidance of commercial interests, who shall tell what may not be the commercial destiny of this country?

This scheme may excite only the curiosity of those who can hardly contemplate it as anything else than an hallucination to amuse for a moment, and then vanish. Nevertheless, such a work will some day be achieved,—if not by a British people, by our neighbours. And let it be remembered, that it is no difficult matter to open a new channel for a new trade, but it is very difficult to change one that is already established.

There is something startling in the proposition of a Railroad to connect the Atlantic and Pacific, and much that will strike

the hasty observer as chimerical, but when we have seen stupen-
dous pyramids raised by the hand of man in the midst of a
desert of shifting sands; when we know that despite the obstacles of nature and the rudeness of art, a semi-barbareous people,
centuries before the Christian era, erected around their empire
a solid barrier of wall, carrying it over the most formidable
mountains, and across rivers on arches, and through the declen-
sions and sinuosities of valleys to the distance of fifteen hundred
miles, let us not insult the enterprize of this enlightened age by
denouncing as visionary and impracticable the plan of a simple
line of rails over a surface of no greater extent, without one-half
the natural obstacies to overcome. To do so would evince a
forgetfulness of the vast achievements of this age. As to its
feasibility, I am aware many will object to it on that ground.
Nevertheless, from all the information obtained, I believe that it
is practicable and easy of accomplishment, and that it can be
accomplished by individual enterprize ; by connecting the sale
and the settlement of the lands on its line with the building of
the road, population must keep pace with the work and be interested in it, and the labour of grading, &c., must pay in part for
the land and make homes for the settlers. The plan or mode
of operation by which it is proposed to carry out this great work
is that the Goverment shall sell, to a chartered company sixty
miles wide of the lands from the Lake to the Pacific, at a reduced rate, or at such a rate as the Government shall pay for
obtaining the surrender to the Crown, from the various bands of
Indians now possessing it. At present it is a wilderness, and
although, to a great extent it is capable of sustaining a large
population, yet it must lie waste and unprofitable, whilst thousands of our fellow countrymen are starving and destitute ; and
so it must remain, without value, and impossible of settlement,
unless some move be made which shall create facilities which
will afford the means of settling these lands, and thus make
them a source of wealth and power to the country. Immediately after such surrender to the Crown, of one hundred or two
hundred miles or more, the route upon it would, be surveyed
and located, preparations made for grading, &c., and proceeding
with the work, a large body of workmen or settlers at once
placed upon it; when ten* miles of the road shall have been

completed, in the most substantial and improved manner, and to the satisfaction of a Commissioner appointed by Government a patent shall issue to the company for the first half of the road or five miles, or patents to the settlers who may have purchased upon the line, as may be deemed most advisable; the Government thus holding still one half of the road. Now, if the sale of land could not be made to produce a sufficient amount to return the money expended on the ten miles of road, then the experiment is the loss of the Company, and the Government would not have lost one shilling, but on the contrary, the five miles of road held by it, must be enhanced in value; if, upon the contrary, the land is raised from beyond its present value to an amount exceeding the outlay, then the half held by Government would have imparted to it an equal increase in value from the same causes, and this ought to be a sufficient security for the due performance of the work. Such should be the proceeding throughout the good or available lands upon the route; but as the road for an immense distance may pass through poor and barren lands—in such case, as much of the nearest good lands beyond the line finished as may cover the outlay upon such a line or section, may be sold by the Company, and patents issued; and when all shall have been completed, the title of the road should vest in the Company, subject to the control of Government, in regulating and fixing tolls, &c. Should the plan fail, Government can lose nothing, because the lands still remain, and their value will have been added to, even by the failure. Thus it is proposed to establish an entirely new system of settlement, on which the hopes for success are based, and on which all depend. The settler on the line of road would, as soon as his house or cabin was up and a crop in, find employment upon the road; when his crop would have ripened, there would be a market at his door, created by those in the same situation as his was the season before, and if he had in the first instance paid for his land, the money would go back to him, either directly or indirectly, for labour and materials furnished for the work, so in one year the settler would have his home, with settlement and civilization surrounding him, a demand for his labour, a market at his door, and, for any surplus of his produce, a railroad to communicate with other markets. The settler who might not have the means to purchase land even at the lowest price, say 3s. 9d. per acre, would obtain those means by his labour on the road and a first crop—he too in one year would have his home, with the same advantages and be as equally independent.

Settlers under any other circumstances, placed in a wilderness, remote from civilization, would have no benefit from the sum paid, beyond his title to the land,—his house built and crop in, he finds no demand for his labour, because all around him are in the same condition as himself; when his crop is grown he has no market; his labor, is true, produces food from the earth, but he cannot exchange it for other different products of industry. A proper and systematic course adopted for inducing immigration from the Mother Country, would relieve her of a surplus population; open the greatest possible extent of wilderness, otherwise forever useless, to settlement and production; making it the means of benefitting and carrying comfort and happiness to thousands of our fellow-subjects in the Mother Country, suffering the worst of evils, caused by too dense population, whilst at the same time such immigration will benefit this country to an illimitable extent. Perhaps it may be thought that the Government of the country should undertake this work, and dispose of the lands as proposed. Private enterprize far exceeds any operations of the Government in celerity, and is much more economical and effective. If the Government undertook it, the sale of the lands would never meet the disbursement, and the difficulties to be encountered by delays in the transaction of the business at the Seat of Government, would alone retard the work and cause it to linger until it perished. Such a work by Government would absorb the entire legislation of the country, and being subject to changes of management and direction at each session, its progress would be utterly defeated; the management of such a great work and the amount of money which this plan could place as a stake to be carried off by the successful party in the struggle, would lead to every species of political corruption and bargaining to secure so vast a prize, which of itself would preclude the selection of the men of the character requisite to carry out the plan; each administration would appoint its own partizans as directors who would exert all the influence that their position, and the immense means at their command would give them, to sustain in power those on whom their offices depended. The only ture way of carrying out this work is by private enterprize connected with the sale of the lands under the protection of Government; or else it must be accomplished by the Imperial Government alone.

The commencement of this work would make it a point of attraction of the whole population of Europe, daily flocking to American shores; most of these are generally without means, nevertheless their labor is the capital which would grade the road, and pay in part for the land. They would not only be interested in the road as a means for their daily bread, but would be sure that its results would benefit their condition, and elevate themselves and families to affluence. Civilization, with all its influences, would march, step by step, with the road, and would draw to it, after the first two years, 100,000 souls annually. Cities, towns and villages would spring up like magic, because the road—the cheap means for the transit of the products of man's labor to a market—would leave a rich reward for that labor, and as it proceeded, produce the further means for the completion of all. The Government, in exchange for the substratum of a suffering population of indigent emigrants of the Mother Country, would find its broad and fertile western territory sprinkled with hamlets and possessing a class of intelligent and happy husbandmen, the best pride and boast of a free country.

It will be at once perceived, that the plan proposed is based upon the assumption that a great portion of the country through which such Railway might pass, is capable of sustaining a large population, and also of furnishing the means of carrying the work over such portions of the line as should be found barren or unfitted for the abode of a civilized man.

I propose now to show that such a description of favourable country exists to an almost unlimited extent, and that westward we have a vast wilderness of land which only requires the application of the labor of the now destitute, to produce abundant means for achieving this great work, richly reward that labor, and open out almost a new world as the inheritance of a British people. I might speculate upon the future, and predict what would be the vast, the mighty results by the acomplishment of this work but it is my object to give a plain statement, which I believe to be based on facts, of the features of the country. There are two points upon Lake Superior from which such Railway might be commenced, each line striking the same point at the Lac La Pluie, a distance about 125 miles, thence to the Lake of the Woods. The one starting at Pigeon River, perhaps, is a more direct route, and I believe in many respects the better one ; the other starts from the Kaministiquia, at the mouth of which stands the Hudson Bay Company's Establishment—Fort William. I will suppose that this latter route is followed, because, without merely asserting my own views and opinions as to its capability of sustaning an agricultural population, I can quote from the published work of another, showing the description and character of country through which I propose to pass proving that at the moment of leaving the shores of Lake Superior we enter a country capable of providing for men all those necessaries and comforts which civilization requires. The Kaministaquia is a large and fine river, but at the distance of about thirty miles up, navigation is obstructed by the Kakabeka Falls, a fall of about 140 feet; the banks of the river are clothed with elm, birch and maple ; above the falls the river is again navigable, to the height of land, which is reached in little over a day's travel by canoes.

The valley of this river is described by Sir George Simpson in his overland journey, and he says :

"One cannot pass through this fair valley without feeling that it is destined sooner or later to become the happy home of civilized men, with their bleating flocks and lowing herds, with their schools and churches, with their full garners and their social hearths. At the time of our visit, the great obstacle in the way of so blessed a consummation, was the hopeless wilderness to the eastward, which seemed to bar forever the march of settlement and cultivation. But that very wilderness, now that is to yield up its long hidden stores, bids fair to remove the very impediments which hitherto it has itself presented. The mines of Lake Superior, besides establishing a continuity of route between the east and west, will find their nearest and cheapest supply of agricultural produce in tho valley of the Kaministiquia."

Through the valley to the height of land, there exist no obstructions which cannot be readily overcome—from this height of land descending to the level of the beautiful Lake of the Thousand Islands, thence to Lac La Pluie and the Lake of the Woods. In reference to this portion, Sir George Simpson says: ' The river which empties Lac La Pluie into the Lake of the Woods, is decidedly the finest stream on the whole route in more than one respect : from Fort Francis (situated on Lac La Pluie) downward a stretch of nearly a hundred miles, it is not interrupted by a single impediment, while yet the current is not strong enough to retard an ascending traveller, nor are the banks less favourable to agriculture than the waters themselves to navigation : resembling the Thames neat Richmond—from the very bank of the river there rises a gentle slope of green sward, crowned in many places with a plentiful growth of birch, poplar, beech, elm, and oak ; is it too much for the eye of philanthropy to discern through the vista of futurity this noble stream, connecting as it does, the fertile shores of two spacious lakes, with crowded steamboats on its bosom, and populous towns upon its borders ? The shores of this latter lake are not less fertile than the other, producing rice in abundance and bringing maize to perfection." The Lakes of the Woods is connected again by a magnificent river 170 miles in length (the Winipeg) with the lake of that name lying to the north-west of the Lake of the Woods—these lakes, with others, being wholly within our own boundaries—the Lake of the Woods is about 80 miles long by 40 broad ; Lake Winipeg is 280 long, and 50 broad. The country in which these lakes are situated is called the Assiniboine, across which flows the Red River, emptying into Lake Winipeg ; upon this river is established the Colony founded by Lord Selkirk. From the western side of the Lake of the Woods, the Winipeg River or Lake Winipeg, any point may be taken, and running directly west not a single obstruction offers for carrying a Railroad to the very foot of the Rocky Mountains, a distance of 800 miles, carrying us through this magnificent country—the Assiniboin, watered by the river of its own name, and by the Red River, each flowing for hundreds of miles ; further westward still we pass through the Saskatchewan country, through which flows the river of that name for 600 miles, navigable for large boats, &c.

Loaded carts traverse this immense country in every direction, and as a proof of how easily all this is accomplished, Sir George Simpson travelled over 600 miles of these plains in 13 days, with 50 horses and loaded carts, and frequently caravans of 200 and 300 carts are traversing these plains, bearing the hunters with their families and equipages, in pursuit of the buffalo, thousands of which animals are destroyed merely for their hides, Sir George Simpson says he has seen ten thousand carcases, lying putrid and infecting the air for miles around in one bed of the valley of the Saskatchewan. The valley of that river alone is equal to the extent of all England ; it abounds in mineral, and, above all the blessings and advantages that can be conferred upon a country like this, is, that coal is abundant and easily obtained ; it crops out in various parts of the valley. Speaking of some portions of this country, through which he was travelling, he says :—" The scenery of the day had been generally a perfect level ; on the east, north and south, there was not a mound or tree to vary the vast expanse of green sward, whilst to the west were the gleaming bays of the winding Assiniboine, separated from each other by wooded points of considerable depth." Again—" The rankness of the vegetation savoured rather of the torrid zone, with its perennial spring, than of the northern wilds, brushing the luxuriant grass with our knees, and the hard ground of the surface was beautifully diversified with a variety of flowers, such as the rose, hyacinth, and tiger lily." Of the Red River Settlement (in the Assiniboine country) he says : The soil is a black mould, producing extraordinary crops, the wheat produced is plump and heavy ; the soil frequently producing 40 bushels to the acre —grain of all kinds is raised in abundance ; beef, mutton, pork, butter, cheese and wool, are productions which likewise abound ; thus shewing that to the foot of the Rocky Mountains, lies a country capable of being rendered the happy homes of millions of inhabitants, when facilities of communication shall be offered which can lead to it." To these statements of Sir George Simpson, might be added those of many others, in corroboration, were it necessary.

That the Rocky Mountains will present a formidable barrier to the construction of a Railway to the Pacific, cannot be denied ; nevertheless I imagine that at the present day, there can scarcely be found any one so bold or rash as to assert, that obstructions will be found to exist which neither the science, skill, nor energy of man can overcome. Let immigration once reach the eastern slopes of the Rocky Mountains, and speedily would vanish all the most formidable obstacles which may now appear to present themselves.

Even now, there are several passes known through those mountains, whereby it may be made practicable to carry steam to the western side. The goods and merchandize required by the Hudson Bay Company for carrying on their trade in the interior, often being landed on the shores of the Pacific, are transported through some of these passes to the eastern side. In his overland journey, Sir George Simpson, ascended from the eastern, crossed, and descended to the Columbia river upon the western side, with forty-five pack-horses, in six or seven days, some days making forty miles a day.

Sir Alexander McKenzie, (at a pass further north) ascended the principal water of the McKenzie River to its head, which he found to be a small lake ; he crossed a beaten track leading over a low ridge of eight hundred and seventeen paces in length, to another lake, this was the head water of Fraser's River which he followed down to where it discharges itself, in the Georgian Gulf or Fuca Straits at 49°, thus showing that a communication between the east and west is open to us.

Wherever the head waters of the rivers on the east and west sides of the Rocky Mountains approach each other, there have been found passes through them.

The Rocky Mountains have been crossed by waggons at various points to the Columbia River, and to the Saptin or southern branch of that river and to the Wallawalla. Thomas P. Farnham, in 1840, crossed to the mouth of the Columbia, and found a waggon which had been run to the Saptin, by an American missionary from Connecticut, and left there under the impression that it could be carried no further through the mountains ; but very soon after that, emigrants going out to Oregon, in 1843, crossed the Rocky Mountains to the Columbia with fifty loaded waggons, performing the journey without any loss or injury, save the bursting of one waggon tire ; and that ought to be sufficient to convince the most sceptical, that a Railroad to, and though the Rocky Mountains, is practicable beyond a doubt, and affording reason to believe that, upon a careful preparatory survey, which must be instituted, new passes through these mountains may be found adapted to the work within our own limits, and on a more direct line with the commodious harbours upon Fuca Straits.

One of the projected lines of Railway communication through the United States was proposed should terminate at Puget Sound. Colonel Fremont one of most scientific men in the United States, was directed to examine and report upon the feasibility of crossing the Rocky Mountains to such terminus. $48\frac{1}{2}°$ N. lat. he examined, and reported its feasibility, stating that " impracticability is not to be named with the subject," either at that point, or even to carry it to San Francisco : "that difficulties from snow would be confined to short spaces, and these inconsiderable.

With reference to the country upon the western side of the mountains, within our boundaries, none perhaps is so well situated for communicating with all the countries and ports washed by the waters of the Pacific. Fuca Straits and the Georgian Sound abound with excellent harbours, without obstruction to ingress or egress at any season of the year ; and are unsurpassed for salubrity of climate, and for advantages are equal to and other country, whether considered under the head of agriculture, commerce, or even the capabilities of becoming a manufacturing one. It holds that position with regard to the Pacific and its islands, which must make it a ruler of its commerce; and when a direct communication shall have been opened from the eastern side of the continent, it must receive the aid of capital and immigration, and rise speedily to an importance scarcely to be parallel.

The Rev. C. G. Nicolay says of this country :—"The growth of timber of all sorts, in the neighbourhood of the De Fuca Straits, adds much to its value as a naval station. Coal is found in the whole western district, but principally shows itself above the surface on the north side of Vancouver's Island. To these sources of commercial wealth, must be added the minerals—iron, lead, tin, &c.; and limestone is plentiful in the north. It will be found to fall short of few countries, either in salubrity of climate, fertility of soil and consequent luxuriance of vegetation and utility of productions, or in the picturesque character of the country.

Thus far I have endeavoured to show the feasibility and expeciency of constructing a Railway to the Pacific, through British territories. I may have failed, in interesting readers in it, sufficiently to exert an influence on the accomplishment of so great a work. Our geographical position gives us advantages and facilities for carring it out which no other country possesses. We are placed so far north, that the climate would protect animal and vegetable productions from injury and destruction, and where the soil, for nearly the entire route, would be capable of sustaining population ; thereby opening to settlement and production the greatest possible extent of wilderness, otherwise forever useless. It is a subject of wide national interest ; one of universal benevolence, opening to mankind the now uncultivated portions of an immense country, to the superabundant population of the Old World, building cities on the silent shores of the Pacific, and growing corn upon the untrodden slopes of the Rocky Mountains. I am aware that many will be found, who will urge the impossibility, and unhesitatingly assert that such a work is impaactible. There never yet was any great work projected, which did not meet with its cavillers or opponents. To such I would reply, there is no work, no enterprise, too vast, too magnificent, if dependent alone upon the labor of man for its accomplishment, aided by the science and skill of the present day.

Within but a short time we have seen a body of 20,000 Mormons traverse a wilderness of 1200 miles, and, seating themselves at the foot of the Rocky Mountains, in one year placed themselves in a most prosperous and flourishing condition: buildingup cities, and, in fact, acquiring the position of an independent State ; who shall tell us, then, that an extensive and systematic mmigration to the fertile lands west of Lake Superior, cannot become equally flourishing, prosperous and happy ? If in the plan proposed there is any merit, it is to be ascribed to Mr. Whitney, of New York. It originated with him, and has become the foundation for many to build upon. In the United States no less than six or seven different projects were brought forward, giving rise to sectional prejudices, and creating diverse interests, which has chiefly been the cause that none of the projected railways has been commenced, unless the one at Panama. Setting aside the advantages to be derived by this country in opening to immigration our western wilds, it will be well to consider whether it is possible, and if possible, whether some one of of the projected routes through the United States be likely to be commenced or built which would be the means of rendering one through our territories useless, for the purposes of controlling the trade of India, &c. I propose to show that not even a ship canal across the Isthmus of Panama, can compete with a communication by the head waters of Lake Superior and the Pacific.

The various routes advocated in the United States, for the construction of a Railway communication connecting the Atlantic and Pacific, are :—

1st. That termed the northern route, from Lake Michigan, terminating at Puget Sound.

2nd. A route from some point upon the Missouri, terminating at the mouth of the Columbia.

3rd. A route from St. Louis, terminating at San Francisco.

4 h. A route from St. Louis, by way of the Gila, terminating at San Diego.

5th. A route from New Orleans across Texas.

6th. Over the Isthmus of Panama, by railroad.

7th. By Tehuantepec or Nicaragua, by ship canal.

The first or northern route is that projected by Mr. Whitney, who explored and examined the country westward of the Lakes Michigan and Superior, for a distance of 800 miles, and compared with the other lines, it has been found to possess the greatest advantages; it pursued a course along $48\frac{1}{2}$ degrees of north latitude, until it terminated at Puget Sound. It was found that thus keeping so far to the north, better lands were offered suitable for agriculture, timber more readily obtained, less difficulty in surmounting the hills, and all the large rivers in a measure avoided, inasmuch as only the head waters of these would be crossed; besides, the distance by this route, 1800 miles, being from 300 to 500 shorter than the others, and the fact that at Puget Sound there always could be obtained supplies of coal from the adjoining British possessions at Fuca Straits. That this or no other particular route has been decided upon by the United States is, I believe, to be solely attributed to the sectional jealousies which the other proposed routes have created, the interest of those advocating the others, requiring a more southerly route, all have been actuated by a fear that their section of the country would not secure its full share of the benefits certain to follow from it. In as great a degree as this proposed northern route has advantages over all the others, so would one through British possessions possess advantages over it.

The more southern lines are all alike liable to the same or similar objections. They would cross a much greater extent of country, where the altitude of the mountains is much greater and large rivers must be crossed, as well as immense tracts of sterile lands which cannot be inhabited; and the want of coal or fuel throughout a very large portion of the line, and at the terminus upon the Pacific, must preclude anything like competition with one throubh British territories where the distance is so very much shortened, where there are less difficulties to overcome, and where the line would pass through some of the best lands in the western country, possessing a fine and healthful climate, and the greater part of which country may be densely populated.

The great barriers upon the American routes, are, upon the one proposed through British possessions, modified or made clear by nature, and above all through the valley of the Saskatchewan, and at the terminus at Fuca Straits abundance of coal is at hand.

A canal across the Isthmus of Panama, at Nicaragua or Tehuantepec, has been mooted for near 200 years; surveys and explorations have been made, but it all rests where it commenced. It is true that this Isthmus forms but a narrow barrier between the two great oceans of the world, nevertheless there are innumerabl obstacles in the way of its becoming the best, cheapest, or quickest route between Europe and Asia.

It is far from being among the most serious objections that the Isthmus of Panama is without harbours upon either side, with shoals and shallow waters difficult of access from either ocean, situated in the latitude subject to calms, squalls, and tornadoes; the climate unhealthy in the extreme, nine months in the year subject to excessive torrents of rain, and the thermometer ranging from 82° to 88°, and the other three months from 90° to 95°, a temperature and climate certain to destroy all animal and vegetable productions, and also to injure greatly all manufactured goods.

In a transportation by Railway across the Isthmus of Panama steam must be used; depôts of coal must become necessary, transported from an immense distance upon the Atlantic side, consequently the rate of freights must be so great as to preclude the transmission of merchandize. Upon the Pacific side depôts of coal would become necessary at the Sandwich Islands or at the Marquesas or Society Islands; the distance from Panama to China, being over 9,000 miles, what steamer could carry freight in addition to her necessary fuel? For such route the cost of the quantity of fuel to be placed at such depôts (a large portion, if not all of it, would most likely be brought from Fuca Straits,) would render the undertaking so unprofitable that it could not compete with the old route round the Cape. Again, the route across the Pacific from Panama, offers many difficulties to sailing vessels in the prevailing winds, calms, &c., so much so that even a vessel might pass around the Cape to China in a shorter space of time than from Panama.

If these objections were not sufficient of themselves to settle the question as to the advantages of the route across the Isthmus of Panama, the distance gained by a route from the head of Lake Superior to Fuca Straits will.

Many, perhaps, who have not reflected upon our position with regard to China, will be surprised to know that here, in Toronto, we are upwards of two thousand miles nearer Canton, than is the Isthmus of Panama to that place; consequently, that through Canada, England can reach the great marts of Asia by a much shorter route than by any other.

Supposing that a ship canal was completed across the Isthmus of Panama, thereby obviating the necessary delays and heavy expenses of transhipment and transit upon a railway, &c., and the steamers passing through that canal of sufficient capacity to carry the fuel required for 9,000 miles, still neither distance nor time can be diminished. Let any one take the map of the world, he will see upon one side of us, Europe at a distance of some 3000 miles, upon the other, Asia at a distance of some 5,000 miles. A line drawn from the great European to the Asiatic marts, passes through our great lakes and across Canada; as we are thus placed in the centre, so may we become the thoroughfare of both.

From London to Panama, 81° of longitudo and 42° of latitude must be overcome, which in a straight line, would vary little from	5,868	miles.
From Panama to Canton, 170° of longitude is to be overcome, measuring 60 miles to a degree	10,200	"
	16,068	
London to Quebec 2,800		
Quebec to Pigeon River, Lake Superior 1,150		
Pigeon River to Fuca Straits 1,500		
Fuca Straits to Canton... 5,400		
	10,850	"
Difference in favour of route through Canada...........................	5,218	"

This, most likely, will strike one as incredible, nevertheless it will be found not very far wrong; and even a much greater difference in favour of Fuca Straits will be found to exist when actual sailing distance is compared, ships often being obliged to run down far to the south or keep up far to the north to catch the winds.

It will be seen that in crossing the globe within the tropics, the degree of longitude measures full 60 miles, where on a course of 30° on a line to 60° latitude, measures but 47 miles to the degree.

	Miles.
Panama to Japan	7,600
Panama to Shanghai	10,600
Panama to Canton	10,000
Panama to Singapore	10,600
Panama to the Sandwich Islands	3,400
Panama to Australia	6,400

Fuca Straits to Japan	4,000
Fuca Straits to Shanghai	5,000
Fuca Straits to Canton	5,400
Fuca Straits to Singapore	7,000
Fuca Straits to the Sandwich Islands	2,400
Fuca Straits to Australia	6,000

As to the advantages of the respective routes, comments are unnecessary, figures and facts settle the question; looking again to the terminus at Fuca Straits, we find advantages as to harbours, climate and position, in a degree commensurate to the disadvantages of Panama, and for steamers, abundance of coal ; the Islands of Japan also abound in coal, where supplies can be had, and if necessary, depôts might be made upon the Aleutian Isles ; no sea is so remarkably adapted to steam navigation as the Pacific, its tranquil surface is scarcely ever agitated by a storm. For sailing vessels, Fuca Straits is equally advantageous, easy of access at all seasons of the year, being out of the latitudes of the prevailing calms ; the passage could be made out and back with the trades ; the course to the great commercial marts of Asia would be west of south, and the north-east trade winds blow almost uninterruptedly, returning by a more northerly route, advantages would be taken of the polar currents which set northward towards Behring Straits, and also of the more variable winds in higher latitudes.

I have thus endeavoured to compare with each other, the different routes proposed for this great highway of the world, to explain the plan by which it is proposed to accomplish it, and to show that the very route which circumstances force us to take, is the only route suitable for the accomplishment of such a magnificent work. British capitalists, it appears, are ready to give their aid towards the construction of a similar communication across the Isthmus of Panama, where must be incurred a much greater expenditure of money than would serve to build the Railway within our territories, and even then, unless nature herself can be overcome, they cannot attain their object ; whilst here, nature invites the enterprise, and where they have no favors to ask of foreign nations, where they will have security that the way shall never be closed to the enterprise of the British merchant, and whereby her possessions upon the Pacific will be secured to Britain for all time to come, and be an additional guarantee for the perpetuity of her dominion upon this continent, it would create a union among all her people which could not be dissolved, with the trade of the world her own forever ; cemented by the affections and undivided interest of her subjects in Europe and in Asia, by means of her Canadian Empire, bound together with sinews of iron.

The view that this opens upon the mind, independent of its internal benefits, staggers speculation with its immensity, and stretches beyond all ordinary rules of calculation. The riches of the most unlimited market in the world would be thrown open to it; and obeying the new impulse thus imparted to it, England's commerce would increase until every billow between us and China bore her meteor flag. By the superior facilities conferred upon us, by our position to control the whole Pacific, and the route through our own country, we would become the common carrier of the world.

Again : Vast countries still lie in the fairy regions of the East, the productions and resources of which are scarcely known to us, and only await the civilizing influence of such a scheme as this to throw down the barriers of prejudice and superstiion. Of this nature and character is the opulent empire of Japan. Through second but to China itself, it holds no intercourse with foreigners, and only permits one nation to land upon its dominions (the Dutch). Ought it to be too much to hope that thus being brought so near to us, some diplomacy or commercial interests would throw its rich markets open to our enterprise.

The cost of the work, even though it should amount to a hundred millions, is no argument to urge against the undertaking which would render every nation on the globe our commercial tributaries. But this is a most extravagant estimate. It would scarcely amount to eight millions, less, indeed, than would be required to cut a canal across the Isthmus of Panama, as is proposed, entailing, perhaps, upon England, some future war, to maintain the rights of her subjects in using such canal, the expenses of which would build a dozen railways; a war that might leave England enfeebled, exhausted, and depressed. The completion of the proposed Railway through British possessions, would find her regenerated with new life, her impulses re-awakened, her energies strengthened, and advancing with a rapidity and vigor that would astonish destiny herself.

The distance from the head of Lake Superior to the Pacific being about 1,500 miles, then allow for detours and crossing the Rocky Mountains, say 250 miles, making in all 1750.

To construct such a road would cost about £5,000 per mile, making a total of £8,750,000.

From the point where it might start upon Lake Superior to Lac la Pluie, would be the most expensive portion upon this side of the Rocky Mountains; from Lac la Pluie onward, the land is of the best quality for the production of food for man, well watered, covered with rich grass, &c. The farmer wants but the plough, the seed, the scythe, and the sickle; at the above rate, ten miles of railway would cost £50,000. Five miles by sixty contain 192,000 acres, the whole of this sold at say 5s. per acre, would not produce the sum required for the bare expense of building, thereby showing that the request for 60 miles is not unreasonable.

Without directing attention to the trade carried on throughout the Pacific, by France, by Holland, and other continental nations, and also by the United States, let us look only to England, it will afford some idea of the incalculable advantages which such a communication would open out through this contry.

Imports into Great Britain from the following ports:

From Bengal, Madras and Bombay, as taken from *Hunt's Merchant's Magazine* for March, 1843, including all to continental Europe, and North and South America, annually,.......... £12,000,000

Less for the amount to France and America,... 2,489,340

£ 9,510,660

From Sumatra and Java (commercial tariff, part 6)...	215,216
The Philippine Isles,..	346,692
New South Wales and Van Diemen's Land (table of revenue, part 12, page 474).............	1,118,088
Mauritius (table of revenue, part 12)	806,593
Chili, estimated at	1,500,000
Peru, estimated at	1,000,000
	£14,497,240
From China the total amount of various productions, teas, silks, &c.,..........................	5,000,000
	£19,497,240

To which must be added the exports from Great Britain, which are sent in exchange for the above productions. The imports and exports of the Dutch East Indies and the French East Indies; should also be considered, as also the exports and imports of the United States ; all would be tributary to such a road.

The Imperial Government have contracted to pay, per annum, for the transmission of a Monthly Mail to Chagres,.......................	£250,000
And from Panama to Callao, for communicating with the Navy in the Pacific,....................	20,000
	£270,000

Having thus alluded to the importance to be attached to the opening of such a communication as proposed with the Pacific, and to the comparative advantages, in a commercial point of view, between it and the Isthmus of Panama, it may not be inappropriate to again advert to it, as regards the effect of the construction of a canal at the latter, would have upon England's maritime supremacy.

As early as the seventeenth century. a company projected by Wm. Patterson, was formed in Scotland, to improve the advantages offered by the Isthmus of Darien, £700,000 was raised, add 1200 men set sail to found a colony, but being denounced by Government, and attacked by a Spanish force, they sunk under accumulated misfortunes, and abandoned the enterprise in despair. The project seems to be again revived, and a Company is now forming in London to carry out the scheme of a ship canal by means of British capital, an almost suicidal act to England's supremacy on the seas, for it would thus contribute to afford superior facilities and advantages to other nations, and particularly to her enterprising rival the United States, from whose rapid strides towards maritime equality England has much to apprehend. Through her geographical position the United States can more readily avail herself of the benefits to be derived from this course than any other nation. Her fleets would steam in one unbroken line through the Gulf of Mexico; her naval power would overawe our settlements upon the north-west coasts; and her influence extend itself throughout all our Indian possessions. The Marquesas Islands, in case the project be carried into effect, lying directly in the route of the navigation to India, would at a step advance into one of the most important maritime ports in the world, whilst the Society Islands, also in the possession of France, would enhance immensely in their value; more than all, returning back; the vessels of Europe would ere long procure their tropical production from the newly awakened Islands in the Pacific Ocean, in just the degree that their value would increase, the West India possessions would depreciate. By changing the route through the Isthmus of Panama, England would voluntarily resign into other hands those commanding maritime and naval stations which she has won at the expense of so much diplomacy, perseverance and wealth. The power and advantages of Saint Helena, Mauritius, Capetown, and the Falkland Islands, commanding the passage round Cape Horn, would be transferred to New Orleans and other cities of the United States bordering upon the Gulf of Mexico, to Cuba, Chagres, Panama, and the Marquesas Islands.

By the present route around the Cape of Good Hope and through the Isthmus of Suez, she has a fair start with the best, and superior chance over most other nations for the Indies, and while her established power and superior marine in that region secures a preponderance in trade, better let well alone, unless she can gain superior advantage.

The commerce of India in every age has been the source of the opulence and power of every nation that has possessed it ; by a silent and almost imperceptible operation, India has been through centuries the secret but active source of the advance of mankind, and while lying apparently inert in her voluptuous clime, has changed the maritime balances of Europe with the visit of every people that has sought the riches of her shores. Her trade imparted the first great impulse to drowsy and timid navigation—it revealed, in the direction of its coasts, region after region before unknown. Like the Genii in the fable, it still offers the casket and the sceptre to those who, unintimidated by the terrors that surround it, are bold enough to adventure to its embrace. In turn Phœnicia, Carthage, Greece, Rome, Venice, Pisa, Genoa, Portugal, Holland, and lastly England, has won and worn this ocean diadem ; Destiny now offers it to us.

APPENDIX No. 2.

Simultaneously with the passage of the Bill for the Incorporation of the Northwest Transportation, Navigation and Railway Company, by the Canadian Legislature, an Act was passed through the Minnesota Legislature, by which this Company will be placed in a most favourable position as regards the trade and traffic of the Western United States.

A BILL for the Encouragement of an International Overland Emigration Route from Minnesota to Puget Sound.

Be it enacted by the Legislature of the State of Minnesota:

SEC. 1. Any Company incorporated by the English or Canadian Governments for the purpose of trade or transportation upon the rivers which form portions of the northern and western boundaries of this State, is hereby authorized and empowered to exercise all the powers conferred by their respective charters within the limits of this State, but upon the express condition that no power thereby exercised shall interfere with any right now held and enjoyed by the citizens of this State, or shall be inconsistent with the Constitution or Laws of this State.

Sec. 2. The authorities of incorporated cities and towns in Minnesota are hereby authorized to appropriate money or guarantee the repayment of sums subscribed and paid by individuals for organizing and furnishing overland parties of exploration during the year 1858 ; but the total amount of such appropriation or guarantee by or on behalf of any single city or town, shall not exceed the sum of three thousand dollars.

Sec. 3. The Governor is hereby authorized and required to compile such reports of overland parties as he may deem proper for public information, and either publish the same during the recess of the Legislature or report at the ensuing session thereon, as he may deem expedient.